HER FIRST CHRISTMAS

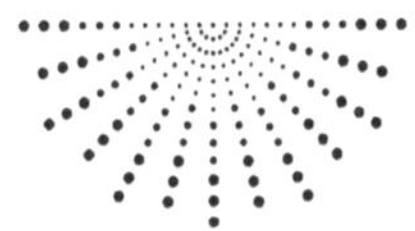

LIBERTY GAINES

PUREREAD.COM

CONTENTS

CHRISTMAS IN JUNE

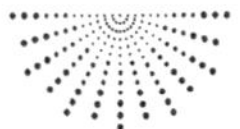

She couldn't stop listening to the Christmas carols that she'd downloaded on her Smartphone. They were the most beautiful songs that twenty-two-year-old Linda Patterson had ever heard and she knew that for as long as she lived, she would never stop playing carols.

Twenty-two years of being in households where Christmas was never celebrated had given her a deep longing for the holidays. Over the years, Linda had promised that when she finally got the chance to celebrate Christmas, she would do it every month.

Well, her chance had come and as she sat on her bed in her bedsitter; she swung her long slender legs to the beat of 'Jingle Bells' and hummed along. It was June but she didn't care, at last she could listen to whatever music she wanted to without fear of being scolded or derided. Her dark eyes were filled with laughter and happiness as she thought about being free and independent at last.

Her rumbling stomach reminded her that she hadn't eaten anything since last night when she came in from yet another fruitless search for a job. If she didn't find one soon, she would have to give up her home, and the thought of that made her sad. She had found this bedsitter quite by accident two months ago, as she was walking in the downtown mall on her day off. Working for Hiram and Nisha Patel as nanny for their two children, Bintu and Anuj, aged six and four respectively, was satisfactory. They gave her a reasonable salary and she had her own small flat above their four-door garage. She had been with them for four years and every Saturday, they gave her the day off. She wanted Sunday but that was the day they entertained their family and friends and needed her services.

That meant that she never got the chance to go to church, not that they would have stopped her had she insisted on going, but she didn't want to be troublesome when they had been good to her. What the Patels did, however, was to ensure that at the time when she would have wanted to attend church, she was very busy with the children.

On that particular Saturday, two months ago, Linda was walking in the mall and ended up in the second basement where there were stores that sold used clothes and shoes. She never shopped anywhere else and as she was perusing through the large boxes filled with different kinds of clothing, she had overheard two store clerks talking.

"Mitch wants me to move in with him, but I don't know," the girl, whose name tag said Terry, was shaking her head. *"I've worked so hard to have my place and giving up my independence and freedom isn't appealing anymore, Sam."*

"Terry, don't you love Mitch?"

"I love him very much, but Mama says we African American girls have to think of being more than just baby mamas and wives to men who might end up not treating us right. And Mama is always right. Do you remember how she stopped me from making a fool of myself three years ago, when I wanted to marry Danny?"

"Don't remind me of that horrid man, Terry. Your mama is a wise woman."

"Exactly. She says that when a woman has financial independence and freedom, she is a force to reckon with. No man would dare mess around with a woman who is in control of the affairs of her own life. That's the reason I don't really feel I should move in with Mitch, at least not yet."

"Mitch is a good guy and he would still allow you to be independent."

"I know that, but what if this thing ends up going nowhere and I have to move out again? It would mean finding a new place to stay, and you know how hard it is to find somewhere as decent as my bedsitter."

"Then why don't you sublease your place for a year, and find out if you really want to be with Mitch for the rest of your life. If things work out, then you can go ahead and give it up. If things go south, then you'll still have your place."

Terry hugged Sam. "That's a great idea. Only trouble is, I don't know who I can sublease the place to. Finding someone who I can trust with my stuff is going to prove difficult."

That was when Linda had stepped in. For twenty-two years, her life had been controlled by others. In fact, that afternoon as she was at the mall, she was thinking about the conversation she had had with her boss. Nisha had *informed her just two days previously that the family was relocating to Ontario where their extended family lived. They wanted Linda to go with them since she was the best nanny they had ever had, and were giving her two days to think about it.*

That morning Nisha had started putting pressure on Linda to say yes, but she asked for time to go to the mall and when she returned, would have an answer for her. Listening to Terry talking to Sam about a woman taking control of her own life made her think. Perhaps it was time for her to take control of the affairs of her life. She was twenty-two and of legal age when she could be in charge of her own destiny and future, and unless she took a step, would always live under the mercy of others.

So, she stepped forward. "I'm sorry that I was eavesdropping on your conversation," she started shyly. "But I couldn't help overhearing what you were discussing. My name is Linda Patterson."

It was Sam who smiled at her. Terry looked at her suspiciously... "Linda, girl, how may we help you? Are you wanting something from the racks?"

"Yes, but that's not why I came up to speak with you. See, I heard Terry saying that she might need someone to sublease her bedsitter to."

"Really? Why would you want to sublease?"

"Because I've never owned my own place before and wouldn't know where to start looking for an apartment or flat. The family I work for as a nanny is relocating to Canada in two weeks' time and want me to go with them."

"Canada, huh!" Terry nodded thoughtfully. "Why won't you go with them? I hear it's a nice place."

"I've read about it too, but you said something that got me thinking. We African American girls need to learn to take control of the affairs of our lives, or something like that. All my life I've had people making decisions for me and I couldn't do anything about it. First my adopted parents, who were killed when I was thirteen, then the orphanage, where I was taken to after that and now my employers. I've never done things for myself and your words have given me a challenge."

"You go, girl," this from Sam, who was beaming from ear-to-ear. "That's my girl!"

"So, when I heard you talking about subleasing, I decided to step forward."

"If your employers are leaving for Canada soon, where will you get the money for rent?"

"I've saved my salary for the last four years and if the rent is reasonable, then maybe I can pay you six months upfront and if after that time, you still allow me to live in *your place, then I'll pay the next six months too. Within that time, I'm sure I'll find a job and I promise that I won't ever give you a problem with the rent and I'll take good care of any stuff you choose to leave behind."*

Terry had asked for references, which Linda was reluctant to supply, since she was quite sure her employers wouldn't give them so willingly now that she wouldn't accept their offer. She was honest enough to tell Terry that, but gave her the number of the housekeeper. She was right about her employers because Nisha went around the house moping like she had lost someone and for the last two weeks that Linda had lived with them, the Patels were very cold towards her. On the day before they were scheduled to fly out, Terry had called and told her that the bedsitter was hers if she still wanted it and she had moved out that same day.

As promised, she had paid Terry six months' rent in advance but that put a huge dent in her savings. She had to find a job or else after six months she would have to find somewhere else to live. Being homeless frightened her and staying at a women's shelter had its own challenges too.

"Dear Lord, please lead me to the place you have reserved for me," she murmured, standing up and walking to the kitchen to find something to eat.

2

AM I IN THE RIGHT PLACE

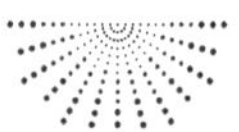

"For the joy of the Lord, shall be my strength," Allan Campbell murmured to himself as he walked to his small office in the basement of Crossroads Christian Fellowship, or CCF as the youth liked to call it. Thankfully, this was Oklahoma and rarely did it get so cold that he needed a heater.

It was the beginning of summer and he was glad he didn't have to don his trench coat, thick socks and gloves anymore. Being a Saturday afternoon, there should be a number of activities going on upstairs but the place was quiet. The music team would be coming in later to practice and that was one group that never missed their sessions. That should have made him happy, but it didn't. The reason the young men and women came at all was just to socialize and also because of the team leader. Osborn Rayder was charming, and even Allan had to admit that the man knew how to lead worship. Unfortunately, the young ladies came to make an impression on him and compete for his attention, regardless of the fact that he was a happily married man with two small children.

Allan sighed as he opened the door of his office and entered. The space was cramped but he didn't complain. His father had always told him that a mature Christian took whatever was dished out to him because it was always the will of God for their lives for that season. This was a tough season for him and he wondered if he would make it all the way to the end.

Being the assistant pastor of a thriving congregation was supposed to make him happy, but he wasn't. As the person in charge of Intercession and Missions Ministries, he wondered if he was truly serving in the right place. Had he really heeded the call of God in his life, or was it his deep sense of adventure that had led him to leave Omaha and the community church where he'd grown up to come out here? Was he really sure that this was what he was called for as a pastor?

His ministries were the hardest to handle because he only had two faithful attendees to the meetings he called for. The senior pastor was even talking about doing away with those particular ministries and reassigning him to be in charge of something else. But his grandfather, Reverend Henry Campbell, had taught him that missions were the backbone of church growth.

"Without new converts, the church might as well be dead. Don't be fooled by a church that is filled with church hoppers. Just the way they hopped into your church, is the same way they will hop out and join another. What a good minister looks for is new converts, people who are hungry to hear the Living Word and learn. Those are the ones who stay with you."

Looking at the present congregation in CCF, Allan had come to the conclusion that most of them were church hoppers according to his grandfather's words. None of them were committed to anything serious, especially where it concerned them spending their time and money. Unless of course, it was for something that would make them popular.

Moving a box of hymn books to the side of his table, he wiped his brow and sat down, opening the large Bible which lay in front of him at a random page and opened Psalm one hundred and twenty-six. He read through it twice, concentrating on the fifth and sixth verses.

"Those who sow in tears shall reap with shouts of joy. He who goes out weeping, bearing the seed for sowing, shall come home with shouts of joy, bringing his sheaves with him."

Allan bowed his head and meditated on the words he was reading. Could it be that he was so caught up in doing the right thing that he was missing what was important? He was doing everything expected of him as the assistant pastor of CCF and head of Intercession and Missions, but was he really praying about the souls he was hoping to win? Was he sowing in tears or in anger? What kind of seed was he sowing?

"Dear Lord, please help me sow the right kind of seed in people's hearts and lives and when the harvest comes, it shall be for the glory of your name."

There was a knock at his door and he bid the person enter. It was Rita Clarke and Allan felt mildly irritated at her intrusion. Rita was one of those people who wasted time going round and round in circles and yet said nothing important. This morning he just didn't have the time to put up with her.

"I thought I'd find you here," she entered his office and stood looking around her, contempt clearly indicated on her face. "Still in the same pigeonhole I see."

"What is it you want?" His voice conveyed its impatience and her eyes narrowed. "I've got work to do, please state what brings you here and leave."

"Oh, I just came to tell you that Devon and I are having a small get together next Saturday for our friends and would like you to come. Please, say you'll come," she used her little girl's voice and Allan held himself back from rolling his eyes. "We need you to come and bless our party."

"Well, sorry, I won't be able to make it because I have something to do next Saturday."

"You're just refusing to come because I left you for Devon, isn't it? You said you'd put all that behind you, but apparently, you're still holding a grudge."

"Rita, it's true that I've put all that behind me and I don't hold any grudge against you. After all, as

Christians, we have to allow the perfect will of God to be done in our lives. In light of what happened, it's obvious that our relationship wasn't in His perfect will. At the time, I didn't understand it that way, but one year is a long time for a person to come to terms with a broken engagement. Besides, I wish you and Brother Devon all the best and if this is what the Lord has planned for you, then may He bless you."

He could see that his words hadn't pleased Rita. She didn't stay for long after that and when she walked out of his office, banging the door as she left, he had a sad smile on his face. Rita Clarke was a beautiful woman; with her light chocolate skin, curly hair and slender frame, she reminded him of Halle Berry. He had fallen in love with her over a year ago, when he first joined CCF. It had taken him almost three months to gather the courage to approach her, especially when he found out that she was the senior pastor's eldest daughter.

Allan was surprised when Reverend Richard Clarke, and his wife, Sophia, welcomed him into the family on the first day that Rita asked him to go for dinner. He only found out much later, after his engagement to Rita ended, that they were so very eager to have their thirty-one-year-old daughter married, that they didn't mind who she brought home to introduce to them.

Without being vain, Allan knew that he was good looking. When he was in Bible School, a friend had told him that he had to be careful about using his looks to charm people in church.

"You've got the most intense brown eyes that I've seen," Naomi Rivers had said. "Be careful never to use them in the wrong way. With those eyes, you can charm birds off the trees, but that isn't who you're supposed to be, Allan. I know for a fact that many of our female classmates are very attracted to you. Remember that when you go out as a pastor, there will be many women in the congregation and the wrong use of the physical features the Good Lord has given you, will cause a lot of people pain."

Allan had been grateful to Naomi for making him take a good look at himself. From that moment, he was careful how he spoke and related to others, especially women and that had stood him in good stead when he became the assistant pastor.

Rita was the first woman he had showed a real interest in, and for days after she accepted his proposal, Allan had walked on air. She was beautiful, intelligent and seemed to be well liked by the congregation. She was just the kind of woman he needed as his wife, to be by his side as he preached the Word of God and brought souls to Christ. He had courted her for three months before proposing and in all that time she was as eager as he was to reach out to the lost and had mobilized many of the youth to join the Missions Ministry.

Things changed when he placed his ring on her finger. Almost overnight, Rita stopped going for missions with him and the number of those who used to accompany them also dwindled until he was left with only two elderly women. No matter how many times he tried to get her to join him again, she always had an excuse. He understood because she was the personal assistant of a senior partner in a law firm, but he always felt like something else was wrong.

Allan believed in a woman being a good wife and mother, but she should also have her own interests. Rita informed him that she was waiting for them to get married and then she would quit her job and be a full-time housewife. After all, her own mother had quit her job as a teacher when she got married to her father. A man needed to take care of his wife and family and provide for her whatever she wanted. That made him a little wary about their relationship and he began to pray about it. The more he prayed, the more he realized that the two of them were quite ill suited.

It was a relief when Rita chose to break off their engagement after one month. "You have no ambition, and I need a man who sees beyond the here and now!" she had screamed as she tossed his ring back at him. "You have no drive and I'm not ready to be a poor pastor's wife, getting the crumbs from others. Papa is prepared to open a church for you if you would just set a date for our wedding, but you've been holding back. Allan, you're not the kind of man I envisioned being married to. See how well my father takes care of my mother. She isn't called the first lady for nothing, he has made her into one."

Allan had refused to be drawn into an argument with Rita and when she walked out, he bowed his head and gave thanks.

A few days later, he saw her with Devon, and though he was angry, he was glad she had shifted her focus away from him. Devon was everything she was looking for, or so she said when they met on the church corridor. He had money, the looks and was able to shower her with so many gifts. He was the perfect man for her.

And now she wanted him to attend the party they were planning, no doubt to rub it in that he was a mere assistant pastor while Devon was a successful businessman. From what little Allan knew about him, Devon's family owned about six gas stations and he managed them all.

Well, he really did have other things to do this coming week, including Saturday.

3

FINDING THE RIGHT PLACE

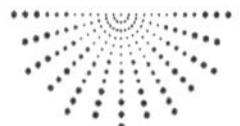

The employment agency that she registered with had no jobs for unskilled workers, but promised that as soon as something came up, they would call her. For two weeks, Linda waited and prayed, and finally the phone call she had been waiting for, came.

"Miss Patterson, we may have an opening for you, but it isn't that great."

"Where is that?" She asked.

"Crossroads Christian Fellowship is looking for an assistant clerk, someone who can read and write and also use a computer. That's what the lady I spoke to said. The work involves filing, being sent on errands and typing programs. Do you think you can do that?"

"I learned how to use the computer when I worked for my former employers but I didn't go to college for that. Will that be a problem?"

"I doubt it, since the lady said most of the work would involve you filing and running errands. I'm sending you there for an interview, which might be just a mere formality but make sure that you present yourself well. This could be the job you've been praying for."

"Thank you so much, Adah. It means a lot to me."

"First, get the job, and you can thank me later. Don't you want to know how much salary you'll be getting?"

"As long as I can pay my bills, that's alright for me."

"Well, considering that it is an assistant clerk's job, the pay isn't much but it will be regular and count this as a way of gaining more experience. In a few months' time, you may be able to get a better job."

"You said the job is at a church?"

"Yes, dear," Adah smiled at Linda. "What do you think, will you take it?'

"Yes, Adah. Let me go for the interview and after that I'll call you and let you know how things went."

"You do that."

Allan was just emerging from his office when someone hailed him. It was Peter Banks, their senior deacon. He was a man in his forties and the only person Allan often interacted with.

"Deacon Banks, what is the matter?"

"Nothing really, I just wanted you to come up to the main offices and meet our new assistant clerk. Remember, we've been looking for someone to fill Regina's place after she left to get married."

"Yes, Deacon. Shall we go up then?"

Linda sat on one of the front pews, eyes roaming around the large church sanctuary. She couldn't believe that she was finally inside a church. Twenty-two-years-old and this was the first time that she was setting foot inside the Lord's house. Why hadn't she thought about coming before?

It was a Wednesday afternoon and the church was empty. She had been interviewed by the deacon and offered the job on the spot, then he left, saying he was going to get the assistant pastor to come and meet her. She couldn't sit still and found herself walking towards the pulpit. It was huge, she'd never seen one quite so huge before in real life. Of course, while she lived with the Patels, once in a while when they weren't home, she would tune into Christian stations and would see the megachurches being built all over America. It had been her desire to one day visit such, and that day had finally come.

She couldn't wait for Sunday so she could come and see the choir that she knew was bound to be fantastic. With a church this size, they obviously had a charismatic choir, with lovely voices and beautiful uniforms. She moved closer to the pulpit and touched it, then closed her eyes to envisage what the service would be like.

And that was how Allan found her when he walked into the church right behind Deacon Banks. His steps faltered and he nearly knocked his leg against one of the aisle seats. It had been a while since he saw someone just standing at the pulpit and seeming to enjoy being in the house of the Lord.

"Miss Linda, I'd like you to meet Pastor Allan Campbell. Pastor, this is Miss Linda Patterson, the lady I was telling you about. She has so graciously accepted our job offer and is now our new assistant clerk."

Allan moved forward with an outstretched hand. Linda placed hers in it, feeling shy all of a sudden. His hand was warm and the first thing that came into her mind was that this was a man who would keep someone safe. She saw a tall man who looked like he played sports a lot, with intense brown eyes and short trimmed dark hair. He had the beginnings of a goatee. He saw a slender and graceful woman with curiosity in her dark eyes. Linda was about three inches shorter than him and her hair was dark, natural and long. It was parted in the middle and held back with a black clip.

"Miss Patterson, welcome to Crossroads Christian Fellowship. I hope you'll enjoy your stay here with us." His voice was deep and pleasant and once again Linda felt that sense of being with someone who would keep others safe. What was it with this man?

"Thank you, Pastor." Linda looked around her. "I've never been inside a church this big. It's so beautiful. I can't wait until Sunday to come and attend service here."

"We not only have services on Sundays, but on Wednesday evenings we have Bible Study, on Thursdays we have prayers for missions and missionaries and on Fridays we visit new converts.

Deacon Banks here can show you around and tell you more about this church."

Peter cleared his throat and shook his head slightly. "Pastor, much as I would like to, I'm late for a meeting with my wife." He turned to Linda. "Miss Patterson, please excuse me. I'll be seeing you tomorrow morning, when I come in."

"Good day, Deacon Banks," Linda and Allan watched as he walked towards the side door.

"I hope you were shown your office," Allan turned to Linda.

"The deacon said he had to come and get you first before he could show me where I'm going to be working."

"Alight then, come this way with me."

RISING AWARENESS

Settling down in CCF was more of a challenge than Linda had first thought. The work wasn't as cut out as Adah had explained. She was also in charge of cleaning the administration offices and there were six of them on the ground floor. The first floor, where the senior pastor had his offices, was off limits to her unless she was specifically asked to go there. Then, she was also charged with the responsibility of opening the church doors on Sundays.

The first Sunday that she attended church, she was so excited. Having been given the keys, she was in church by seven even though Pastor Allan had told her that the service normally began at nine-thirty. She sat down in one of the front pews and waited for the other members of the congregation. Allan came in ten minutes later and after half an hour two elderly women arrived. Allan introduced them as Nancy Summers and Jane Porter.

No one else arrived for at least an hour, but by that time the four of them had had a prayer session that Allan felt was quite satisfactory. He hoped Linda wouldn't drop by the wayside like so many others who'd started off so well. People would join the church and be so excited about the different programs going on and would serve diligently for a while. But then a short while later and attendance would begin to dwindle and then stop altogether, even though they still attended Sunday service without fail.

Linda found herself wanting to be in church all the time and she thought she was going crazy. Could a person be faulted for wanting to spend so much time in the house of the Lord? It was as though she had an insatiable hunger to hear about the gospel.

"Sister Linda, is this the first time you're becoming a member of a church?" Nancy Summers asked her that evening when they met for their weekly Bible Study. "You have such a passion that I haven't seen in a long time."

Linda laughed softly. "You could say that."

"Why is that, child?" This came from Jane Porter. The three of them were waiting for Allan to join them so they could begin the Bible Study.

"My biological mother abandoned me in a hospital immediately after giving birth to me and I was adopted by the people who gave me my name. Mr. Mitchell and Mrs. Hilda Patterson were kind parents but they were atheists. We never went to church and they didn't allow anything about Christianity to cross the threshold of their house. We never ever celebrated Christmas or Easter."

The two women looked at her, incredulous looks in their eyes. "What?" Jane finally burst out. "You never celebrated Christmas and yet you're in America?"

Linda shrugged. "What I know about Christmas, I learned from my friends at school. On my thirteenth birthday, the Pattersons were killed in an accident. They were going to get my birthday cake and it was drizzling. A truck lost control on the highway and there was a pile up." She twisted her lips sadly. Much as they had been strict and didn't allow her to go to church, the Pattersons had been good parents. Unfortunately, at the time of their death they hadn't left any will so Mitchell's brother took over his business, house and other properties. He and his wife hadn't wanted Linda so she was sent to an orphanage.

"Don't orphanages have chapels or something like that? Or at least allow children to go to church?"

"Not the one I was brought up in. They weren't atheists but they weren't into Christianity either. None of the wardens encouraged us to go to church, they just weren't interested. Then I turned eighteen and got a job as a nanny for a Hindu couple. Once again going to church and the Bible were banned from their house. You know something?" The two women shook their heads. "I've never celebrated Christmas and this one is going to be my first, so I'm really looking forward to it."

Nancy stretched out a hand and touched Linda's arm. "What you're saying sounds like a joke or a dream. I've never thought about those who aren't as privileged as we are. I can't begin to imagine living year after year without celebrating the birth of our Lord and Savior, and His death to save us from sin."

Linda was puzzled. "Sometimes, when the Patels weren't at home, I would tune into one of the Christian stations and they always talked about being born again. Isn't it automatic that when a person begins attending church that they are a Christian?"

"No, my child," Nancy shook her head. "Going to church or being a member of one doesn't make you a Christian. That status is only obtained when a person gives their life to the Lord. You believe in your heart that He came and died for your sins, then you confess with your mouth that you're a sinner in need of grace. That's what being born again means."

Linda listened so keenly as the two women explained salvation to her. When Allan walked into the church sanctuary for Bible Study, he found Linda on her knees. She was weeping but there was such peace on her face that he was taken back to the time when he first accepted Christ into his heart. There was no Bible Study that day and after praying and counseling with Linda, the three hugged her and their meeting broke up. Allan gave her a new Bible as a gift for joining the family of God.

She walked home, her new Bible clutched in her hand and she slept while holding it close. Of all the presents she had received over the years, none was as precious as this one and for the next few weeks when she wasn't busy, she would read as many verses as she could. She started from Genesis but by the time she got to Exodus she was getting confused.

None of it made much sense to her and she knew she had to ask for help.

The best person to ask for help was Pastor Allan, but she was shy of being with him alone. When Nancy and Jane were present it was easy to have a discussion and talk about anything under the sun. But she had never had to hold a personal session with Allan and she didn't know how she was going to approach him. She had seen how many ladies in church hovered around him, and once in a while she acted as the receptionist. The church phone never stopped ringing and it was always one lady or the other, asking to speak to Allan. He didn't own a cellphone because he said they were more trouble than help, and anyone who needed to speak to him had to use the church line.

Linda's fear was that if she sought Allan out for a one on one session, he might think she was using that as an excuse to flock around him. She really needed to find answers before her head exploded.

Allan found himself thinking about the new convert who was also the assistant clerk, more than he should. Even when he was dating Rita, he never spent so much time day dreaming about her and he wondered what was so special about Linda Patterson.

From the moment she had become a Christian, she seemed to have an insatiable quest for knowledge of the things of God. Never had he met someone who hungered so much for the Word, but she also seemed to be confused. He wondered why she didn't come to him for help when he could help her. Many times, he saw the look in her eyes as if she wanted to ask him something, but then she would quickly turn her head away when she noticed him looking at her intensely.

The best thing to do would be to ask her whether she had any questions, and that is what he did that evening when they met for Missions ministry.

"Sister Linda, I notice that you seem a little tense and confused, is there anything you wish to ask us?"

Linda sighed and then nodded. "Pastor Allan, I've been reading the Bible and started at Genesis. I have reached Exodus around the fifteenth chapter and it is all so confusing to me."

"You know that I'm always in my office, why haven't you come to ask for help?"

Jane shook her head. "Pastor, with all that is going on in church and the scandals that are rocking the Body of Christ, it isn't wise for you to ask Linda to come and see you in your office. First of all, you're in the basement and that is quite secluded. Not everyone will see your meeting down there as innocent and you know that we don't want the Lord's name to be mocked. Remember when you were dating Rita, we advised you against allowing her to come to your office. For a while people spoke ill about you but luckily, her father, our senior pastor intervened and all that died down. We need to be careful about how we conduct ourselves as Christians."

Allan nodded. "Thank you, Sister Jane. Just to be clear, I didn't intend for Sister Linda to be meeting with me in the basement, but here in the sanctuary, unless there will also be a problem with that? Like you say, all we do must be above reproach so we shall not bring shame to the name of our Dear Lord."

"Meeting here in the sanctuary is good because at least there's always someone coming in or going out, but still choose the time wisely and carefully. Since you both work here, the thing I would suggest you do is meet at lunch time when we're also here for midday prayers. In that way, no one will think suspicious thoughts," Nancy said. "After all, it's not like you're discussing anything else other than the Word of God, so our company shouldn't be a problem."

"It won't be, Sister Nancy. That is of course, as long as Linda is comfortable with the arrangements."

"That is alright," Linda said, feeling relieved and bereft at the same time. She had been looking forward to spending some time alone with Allan but this was a wise way to handle things. She knew that she was deeply attracted to him but being such a charismatic young man, she was aware that he didn't think of her in those terms at all. Having a meeting with the two elderly ladies would ensure she never made a fool of herself.

BEGINNING THE MISSION

"I just needed to ask something of this small group of ours," Linda looked around. Autumn was here and they were holding their meeting in the gazebo in the church garden since the sanctuary was being renovated in preparation for Christmas.

"Yes, Linda." Jane spoke for the rest of them.

"I told Jane and Linda about the orphanage where I grew up. Precious Gems was my home for five years and in all that time, nobody introduced Christ to me, no one spoke about the Bible. For the past four months that I've worked here, I've received such deep blessings that I want to share them with those who brought me up. I feel like a child who has found priceless treasure and wants to share it with her parents and the rest of the family."

Nancy nodded. "That's a good idea, but will the wardens or administration of the orphanage allow us to speak to the children and anyone else about Christ? They may not give us the chance."

"Last week I went there and met the senior warden. It's still the same woman who was there at the time I was leaving four years ago. Mrs. Donna Wright is fairly open minded. I called and asked her if it would be alright for me to bring some friends to speak to the children about Christ and salvation, and she said it was alright as long as we don't make a circus out of it."

"What did she mean by a circus?"

"Jane, don't tell me you haven't seen what some of our fellow brethren do when they visit a place like an orphanage or women's shelter. It becomes all about them and what they are doing for the residents that it turns out into something unpleasant." Nancy turned to Linda. "Please reassure the warden that there's only four of us and we will hold our meetings very quietly and disturb no one. We belong to Missions Ministry and it's about time that we started reaching out to others. We're few, but with unity we will accomplish much. Pastor Allan, what do you think?"

"We're together in the Spirit. I've been praying for the Lord to open a field for us to go in and either sow seed or else harvest what others who went before us sowed. Now this door is open to us, we need to make a move soon enough before the devil comes in with his wiles and keeps us out. People change their minds and my grandfather loves to say that we should grab every opportunity we can get to bring as many into the family of God as we possibly can."

"Which is the best day for the orphanage?"

"It's Saturday from two until five. While I was there, that was the time allocated as personal time and the children are allowed to do whatever they want. All the other times they are so busy."

"Then Saturday afternoon it shall be, Linda," Jane turned to the others. "Any objections?"

There were none and that Saturday found them at Precious Gems Orphanage. Though the reception they received from the senior warden was lukewarm, they went away feeling that indeed, this was a door that had opened for them.

The next week on Tuesday, as Linda was getting ready to take her lunch break, Jane walked into her office. "My dear," she hugged her. "I can't stay for long because Nancy and I are going to the mall. Her daughter is getting married in New York in two days' time and she has asked me to accompany her. Since it's a last minute thing, we have to find something to wear. But don't fear, we'll fly back in time for Saturday's evangelistic mission to Precious Gems. Pass our apologies to Pastor Allan."

"I'll do that and I hope you both have a wonderful time. I'm sorry I don't usually carry much money on me, but please see if you can find something for about twenty dollars as my gift to the couple. And send my love and congratulations to Nancy and her daughter." She pulled her purse from under her desk and handed Jane twenty dollars.

"You're a good girl," Jane touched her cheek. "One day soon, the Lord will remember and bring a good man your way. Just you wait and see, and then it will be your turn to rejoice."

"Amen." Linda walked into the sanctuary with a smile on her face. It was true that she wished Nancy's daughter all the best. As the assistant clerk, she was once in a while called upon to type wedding programs and each time she did, she wondered when her own turn would come.

"Somebody looks happy," Allan told her immediately she sat down. "What's going on, Linda?"

"Pastor, Jane has just been to my office to excuse her and Nancy. They're going to the mall to buy clothes for Nancy's daughter's wedding which is being held in New York. They sent their apologies."

"Nancy had told me about it, but I didn't think it would be this soon. Well, shall we begin then?"

"Yes, Pastor."

"When we're alone, would you call me Allan, please?"

"I …." Linda was at a loss for words.

"Never mind, whatever is comfortable for you. Let's pray."

Linda was glad when their lunchtime session ended. She'd never been so aware of a man before and she felt guilty about thinking wrong thoughts about the man of God. What was wrong with her? Allan was a nice man who took his calling as pastor very seriously and didn't play around. In all the time she'd been at CCF she hadn't heard any scandal attached to him, except of course, his engagement that ended a year ago.

She knew Rita because the lady flaunted the gifts that her rich boyfriend gave her. He had even bought her a car and she wouldn't stop talking about how lucky she was to have a man who really cared and knew how to take care of a woman.

Linda felt sad for Allan because she could see that what Rita did sometimes affected him and he would be tense the whole day. Sundays were especially worse because Rita would come into the sanctuary on Devon's arm and sit in the front pew, sometimes next to Allan and sometimes in front of him. It couldn't be easy having to see the woman he was once engaged to, now with another man, and she sympathized with him.

When Linda returned to her office she wouldn't stop thinking about Allan and how he was really dedicated to the work that he did. He never missed a day of prayer, not even when he was ill. Two weeks ago, he'd had a terrible cold and couldn't stop sneezing. His eyes were running so that he looked like he was crying, but he insisted on leading Bible Study. It was Jane who sent him home and promised that they would be by later to check on him and also to bring him some chicken soup.

The three of them went to visit him that evening and that was the first time Linda had been to Allan's apartment. It was about three blocks from the church and had two bedrooms. They found him asleep on the couch in his living room and since Nancy had the keys to his apartment, they had simply dropped the chicken soup and hot rolls and left.

She was still daydreaming when she noticed that Allan was standing in front of her desk. "You seemed so far away and distracted today, is everything alright?"

"I'm sorry, I've just got a lot on my mind. Hope I didn't inconvenience you."

"You didn't, but I pray that whatever is disturbing you is temporary. I was thinking that perhaps we should stop the lunch time meetings since you're doing well, and instead, concentrate on the evening ones. In that way, you won't be too tired to pay attention."

"We'll have to discuss that with Nancy and Jane when they're back."

"Of course, Linda. I just wanted to run it by you before bringing it up in our next meeting."

"Your suggestion is alright." But even as she said it, Linda was feeling like she was losing something. Those moments spent in Allan's company even with Nancy and Jane around, were special for her. He was a good teacher and had a soothing voice. She also liked him because he didn't dress flamboyantly like their senior pastor, but toned down his wardrobe. At least they would still have their evening meetings.

IMPORTANT VERSUS RIGHT

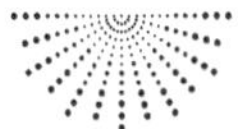

"Three weeks to Christmas, Linda," Maryanne, the church secretary, called out to her on her way to lunch. "In three weeks' time you'll celebrate your first Christmas, I mean really celebrate. Here at CCF we usually have a wonderful time."

"What goes on?"

"You've seen all the renovations that were done to the sanctuary?" Linda nodded. "Our Senior Pastor Clarke wants this to be a Christmas with a boom, his words not mine. Usually the church hires outside caterers so all of us have a wonderful time. Then, a week before Christmas, we'll all be asked to pick out a piece of paper from a basket. You're to buy a special gift for the person whose name you've picked, and Senior Pastor says it should never be less than fifty dollars. For the past three years that I've been here, I've received a microwave oven, a toaster and a percolator. Just the things I was praying for."

Linda listened with a half ear as her colleague went on and on about the lavish Christmases celebrated at CCF.

"Reverend Clarke said this year he wants all of Oklahoma City to know that CCF has made huge strides and is the place to be. We're hoping to attract as many youth as we can and so fill our church. It will be so exciting."

"Well, that is certainly something to look forward to," Linda knew deep down in her heart that she wouldn't be attending Christmas celebrations at CCF. She'd already made other plans and was just glad that she wouldn't be there because she couldn't afford to spend fifty dollars on a gift for a person she hardly knew. If it was all about buying gifts for people specifically and handing them over to them, then she would gladly do so. The only people she would be sending cards to or buying gifts for were Allan, Nancy, Jane, Maryanne and Timothy over in the accounts office. Those were the ones she knew very well and wouldn't feel uncomfortable giving gifts to.

"It certainly is, you'll love all that will be going on. Last year there was so much food left over that anyone who wanted to, carried takeaway boxes. Mine lasted until New Year's Day. That's how good it was."

"Just out of curiosity, where does the church get all that money to spend on Christmas? The offerings and tithes?"

Maryanne shook her head. "Reverend Clarke would never use church money for that. Instead, all of us contribute and you'd be surprised at how wealthy some of the members are. Next week when the letters inviting donations go out, you'll see from the list just who is who. The advantage of a big church is that there are members who fully support the work of the Lord."

Linda wondered how giving money for a lavish party entailed supporting the work of the Lord.

Allan was thinking the very same thing as he sat in his basement office. Jane had expressed her disapproval at the amount of money being spent to renovate the main sanctuary, yet the assistant pastor of the church had a rabbit hole for an office.

"During the next church meeting, I'll express my disappointment at the way we often concentrate on the

mundane and leave out the important. This is abominable."

"Sister Jane, those are very strong words. There's no problem with renovating the church and making it better."

"I don't disagree, Pastor. What saddens me is that you should be in this small office that is also used as a storage room instead of being given a larger one above ground. It's a good thing the weather in Oklahoma is warm, or else we would find you frozen to death down here in the winter. It just isn't right and no matter what you say, the board has to give me a satisfactory answer."

Allan didn't want any trouble because he was content enough with his office. In any case, he hardly spent time there because whenever a church member needed to be counseled or to speak to him, they met in the sanctuary or else the private lounge next to Reverend Clarke's office. Someone had once suggested that this be turned into an office for the assistant pastor but it had brought about a huge argument and the matter was dropped. Many members felt that their senior pastor deserved to have a place where he could meet with his special guests in private. What's more, the first lady of the church used this as her own room whenever she needed to.

"Lord, help us all see what we're doing so we can pick out what needs to be done as opposed to what we want to do."

According to him, all of them had their priorities wrong. Celebrating Christmas wasn't wrong in itself, but his grandfather had told him it certainly wasn't the time to buy each other expensive gifts and eat gluttonously. Christmas was the time to reflect on how the Lord left His glory and came to a fallen earth, being born in a dirty manger. It was the time to remember those who were less fortunate and bestow gifts to them sacrificially. It was the time to think about others and not oneself, and he wondered if Linda would be attending the Christmas Day party at the church. She hadn't said anything about her plans and he kept thinking about how she should spend the first Christmas she was celebrating. It deserved something special, not just eating, drinking and making merry.

He got the chance to ask her that evening as she finished work and was walking home. He was waiting and fell in step beside her. "Linda, I hope you had a good day today."

"I did," she sighed. "Maryanne was just telling me about Christmas and what goes on around here. It sounds nice," there was caution in her tone.

"But? Just say it. Something is troubling you about all this."

"I don't mean to be a party pooper but what you've taught me about Jesus shows that He gave of Himself and didn't take from people. I can't understand why such pomp has to be on display on the Savior's birthday. Those are just my thoughts and I'm sorry to express them."

"Will you be attending the party?"

Linda shook her head. "I already promised the warden at Precious Gems that I would be celebrating Christmas with them. I'd love for the children to learn that Christmas is all about caring for the needs of others. I've already prepared my letter to excuse myself from the celebrations, since Maryanne told me invitations were to be sent out next week."

"You say that you'll be at the orphanage, may I join you there?"

Linda turned and looked at him in surprise. "Why? You're the assistant pastor here and should be involved in the activities of the church. What will people think of you if you're not there?"

Allan smiled, "It doesn't matter what people think, it's what my conscience tells me. Right now it's telling me that eating and drinking isn't right. Sharing my day with those little ones is what counts. I'm sure Nancy and Jane feel the same way, because they mentioned something like baking a cake for the children. I've been here for two Christmases and both times the two lovely ladies didn't attend the celebrations with everyone else. If we invite them, I'm sure they'd love to join us. We can then make Christmas special for the children at Precious Gems."

"Well, as long as it doesn't get you in trouble with the other members of the church leadership. The senior pastor and deacons' board may not take too kindly to your not attending the celebrations. It might not bode well for you."

"If I have to lose my job for doing the right thing then so be it. This is the Lord's work and if my season here comes to an end, He will most definitely open another field where I may serve. Don't be worried on my account."

7

FACING THE PAST

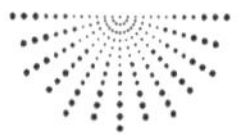

llan was ironing his shirts for the next week when his buzzer went off. Nancy had come in on Saturday morning after returning from New York to clean and had also done the laundry. He'd come home straight from church after service that Sunday because he wanted to tidy his house up. When he found out that it was Rita waiting downstairs, he hastily donned the light cotton shirt that he had discarded as he did his ironing. Allan's rule was to never let any woman who wasn't closely related to him into his house, especially when she came alone. The only person who had a key to his apartment was Nancy and it was because once a week she came by to clean it.

He decided to go downstairs rather than have her come to his apartment and when she saw him, she got angry that he hadn't invited her into his house. She was further incensed when he insisted on taking her to the nearby café for a cup of coffee.

"You're not being fair to me," she sobbed into her handkerchief immediately after they sat down at a table for two. The waitress, whose name tag read Lucy, hovered around. He asked for two white cappuccinos and then turned back to Rita.

"I don't understand what you're saying and why you feel that I'm not being fair to you."

"You don't love me anymore and don't seem to care about my feelings at all."

Allan frowned, wondering if he was dreaming or if this was a test. "Rita, you ended our engagement a year ago, and said I wasn't the man you wanted. What's going on now? Besides, you've moved on with your life and I've never stood in your way."

"Devon and I broke up because he claims that I still love you and I'm obsessed with getting you back," she wept.

"I'm really sorry to hear that, but I don't think I'm the right person you should be talking to right now."

"You see," she raised a tear streaked face to him. "You're not even moved by my pain, yet I still love you. Why are you doing this to me, Allan?"

Allan shook his head slowly. "Rita, to be honest, I'm really confused and I still don't understand why you've come to me at this time."

"It's because of her, isn't it?" Allan didn't respond immediately because the waitress returned with their beverages. He picked up his cup and took a sip before raising his eyes to her.

"Who?"

"That clerk in church. You've been spending so much time with her and even going on dates. You thought I wouldn't find out, didn't you?"

"Rita, you're making a scene and green isn't a good color on you. Stop being all dramatic and take your coffee. Leave Linda Patterson out of this because it has nothing to do with her. If your spies didn't tell you, each time Linda and I go out, as you claim, Nancy Summers and Jane Porter are always with us. We belong to the Missions Ministry and have our days to evangelize. If you doubt what I'm saying, why don't you join us this Saturday to see where we go and what we're up to?"

"People are talking that you spend so much time together," she repeated and he sighed inwardly. This was going to be difficult, but he didn't owe her any explanations. Still, he had to be cautious about how he told her that she had to leave him alone. Rita was very unpredictable and she could turn around and vent all her rage on Linda, who didn't deserve any of that.

"You shouldn't pay attention to what people say, Rita. I have a lot of work to do and don't want to get into an argument with you. Please, find someone who can counsel you because I'm not the right person. We were too close at one time for me to be impartial."

"Allan, you've said it. We were close, why can't we be again? I missed you so much in this past one year and I'm willing to let go of the past and your failings so we can move forward."

Allan stared at her incredulously, laughter welling up within him. "My failings?" He shook his head. "Rita, this isn't the time and place. If we have to speak then let it be in church, where we won't be tempted to exchange bitter words. I respect your parents too much for that."

She left after another flood of tears, her coffee untouched. He watched as she drove away in the car that Devon had bought her, wondering what had just happened.

On Monday morning when Allan got to work, there was a message waiting for him at the receptionist's desk. Linda was filling in for Brenda White who Allan remembered had started her maternity leave.

"Did you have a lovely weekend, Linda?"

"Yes," she smiled and he felt butterflies in his stomach. This was one beautiful woman inside and out and even though she didn't dress up like the other ladies in church, she had an inner glow that outshone all of them. He was in love with Linda Patterson! "How was yours?"

"Did the laundry, fed my eighty-six-year-old neighbor's cat and emptied the trash. That sums it up. That's how I spent my Sunday afternoon."

"Before you go down to your office, Reverend Clarke and Mrs. Sophia would like to have a word with you upstairs."

"Do you know…" he shook his head. "Never mind, would you watch my briefcase while I go up?"

"No problem, I'll put it under the desk so that if you return and I'm not here, you can easily find it."

"Thank you."

As Allan took the elevator to the first floor office of the senior pastor, he couldn't help but wonder if this meeting had anything to do with his conversation with Rita the previous day. Well, he was about to find out. Adjusting his tie, he knocked and was bid to enter.

"Allan," Richard came towards him, both hands outstretched. He was a huge man, taller than Allan by about two inches and well built. He kept fit and Allan knew that he spent a lot of time in the gym. "It's been a while since we had a talk, you and I. How have you been?"

"I'm doing alright, Reverend Clarke." They shook hands then he turned to Sophia. "Mrs. Clarke." She was seated on the large couch in her husband's office. There was another seat opposite hers and he walked towards it, but waited to be asked to sit.

"Allan, it's good to see you." The chill in her tone belied her words and he sighed inwardly. Sophia

Clarke was a beautiful woman, her daughter had taken after her. There wasn't a hair out of place and her perfume filled the whole office. In the time that he had known her, Allan knew that she also had moods that changed with whatever was going on. One moment she could be loving and caring, but she could also be very cold and forbidding. "Sit down," she made it sound like an order and he nearly refused to do so. He didn't like it when people patronized him, but these were his seniors and he did so.

"We've called you here because we're concerned at some disturbing news that has reached us. I know that we've been away planting churches around the country, but we still know what goes on at our home church." Allan was silent, waiting to hear more. Richard also expected him to make a comment and when he didn't, he turned to his wife. "Honey, do you want to take it from here?"

"No, my love. Just carry on," she waved a perfectly manicured hand at him.

"Allan," Richard sat down beside his wife and looked at Allan. "You're like my son, and it broke our hearts when you ended your engagement to our daughter." Allan was surprised to hear this. "At the time, we put it down to the extra work that you were doing.

Rita told us you weren't paying attention to her as before and when she wanted to know why, you ended the engagement. You hurt my little girl but I chose to forgive and let things be. Now you're doing it again. Why are you making my little girl miserable?"

"Reverend, I don't understand."

"What's going on between you and Linda Patterson, the clerk downstairs?"

"How do you mean?"

Sophia made an impatient sound. "Don't act dumb, Allan. You know perfectly well what my husband is referring to. The two of you have been spending so much time together without caring that others see you. Where have you been going with Linda?"

Allan sat back and observed husband and wife, wondering if he should even bother defending himself. He decided to do it for Linda because he didn't want her brought into the matter. "Did your sources also tell you that Jane Porter and Nancy Summers have always gone out with us? As you're both aware, I'm in charge of Missions and Intercession. We have prayers together and also started evangelizing to the children and wardens of Precious Gems Children's Orphanage. If you need proof of this, I'll give you the senior warden's number."

"While your explanation sounds plausible, it still doesn't say why you have to be with Linda every Saturday. Don't you have other duties here at the church?"

"With all due respect, Reverend. I was called to be a fisher of men and to make disciples of those who believe so as to fulfill the Great Commission of our Lord Jesus Christ. Christianity is all about making disciples and training people to impact the world for Christ, and for that I make no apologies." Allan was feeling angry but he restrained himself from lashing out. He respected Richard and Sophia and besides, they were servants of the Lord and deserved his honor. "If evangelizing is doing the wrong thing, then I will hand in my resignation letter as soon as I go down to my office and write it. I will resign from my job as assistant pastor with immediate effect."

"It hasn't come to that," Richard was alarmed.

"If you remember, it was your daughter, Rita, who broke off our engagement. She said I didn't have the ambition and drive to be rich and famous like her father. Who can compete with that, sir?" Allan wasn't sure, but he saw something akin to respect in

Sophia's eyes. "May I please be excused now, unless there's something else?"

Both of them shook their heads and he thanked them and walked out. He stood outside the closed door and took a deep breath. No one needed to know how angry he was feeling right now, and when he presented himself at Linda's desk to collect his briefcase, he was smiling.

8

MAKING THE RIGHT CHOICE

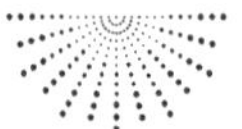

Sophia Clarke couldn't sleep so she woke up and went to the balcony of their bedroom. She had it all; a wonderful husband, thriving ministry and two beautiful daughters. She was really the first lady of CCF and people treated her with respect. She should be happy but she wasn't. Allan Campbell's words had pierced her heart and she found herself weeping silently.

Richard slipped his hands around his wife from behind and she leaned against his chest. "So, you couldn't sleep either?" She shook her head. "I couldn't stop thinking about what Allan said."

Sophia turned around to face her husband. "He was right and I feel terrible about the way I wanted to rip him apart for making our daughter sad. Allan is a good boy and it's true, Rita was the one who broke off their engagement. A few days later she started running around with that Devon boy. We allowed our blindness to our daughter's faults to take over and I feel that we owe Allan an apology."

"Indeed, we do," Richard sighed. "But that's not all. When he talked about his calling, I felt the years rolling back to when we were first called. Remember how we were so passionate for the Lord and never spent a single day without telling at least one person about Christ? Rita was nearly born on the road as we were on our way to a crusade, remember that?"

Sophia gave a small sob, nodding. "We forgot why we were called in the first place," she put her head on her husband's chest and wept. He gently rubbed her shoulder. "I feel so terrible at how much I've let the Lord down. Remember how we promised that we wouldn't become one of those pompous pastors, yet that's exactly what we are. Richard, what have we done to the church of Jesus Christ and to ourselves?"

"God has been merciful to us. I've had no peace since we spoke with Allan and I believe this is our wake up call. We've enjoyed grace all these years, and yet we wanted to interfere in another servant of God's calling. I'm deeply ashamed of myself."

They stood in silence, holding each other and looking over their city. "I remember when we bought this house from that lovely missionary couple who went to Africa. The Sanders said they were selling the house to us only because we're servants of God. Reuben said he and Elsie stood on this balcony every night at three, looking down at Oklahoma City and praying over it. They called themselves the watchmen of Oklahoma City and we promised that we would do the same. Yet we've allowed ourselves to stray from our calling and got involved in the mundane. What are we going to do?" It was a cry from her heart and touched her husband.

"Baby, don't cry. There's something we can do."

"What?"

"Christmas is in a few days' time. We've taught our congregation to be selfish and greedy, same as we've been. This year it won't be business as usual." Sophia nodded. "This year and in years to come, we're going to teach our flock the true meaning of Christmas. No more lavish parties and exchanging expensive gifts. I feel so small and useless."

"May God guide us on what to do."

"Amen."

Allan was summoned to Richard's office for the second time in just a matter of a few days. He was so sure that he was going to be asked to resign from his job that when the couple apologized to him, he stared at them for almost a full minute before responding.

"You're not asking me to resign from being assistant pastor?"

"Not at all. You're a good servant of God and this is where you should be," Sophia said. "We're sorry for making you feel as though you don't belong here. We've also spoken to our daughter and she won't be causing you any more trouble. She's decided to go to my sister in New York when the New Year comes, so that ends all that."

"Thank you so much," Allan truly loved this congregation, even with all their shortcomings. He wasn't perfect either and he felt that given another chance, he would do things differently.

Richard came and shook his hand, "Well, have a wonderful day then, Allan."

He stood up and turned to leave, then remembered something. "Reverend Clarke, Mrs. Sophia."

"Yes?" They both responded, looking up at him.

"May I please excuse myself from this year's Christmas celebrations? Linda, Jane and I have been evangelizing at Precious Gems Orphanage and we promised to celebrate Christmas with the children. It was Linda who actually promised, but I asked if I could go along and so did Jane and Nancy. When she said yes, I made a promise to be by her side on this particular mission. May I please be excused?"

"Yes. Follow your heart, Allan, and never make any apologies for doing the Lord's work. That's your calling and may you never forget it."

"Thank you, Mrs. Sophia. I'll be leaving now."

9

NOT BUSINESS AS USUAL

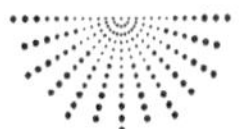

Linda woke up with a huge smile on her face. Christmas Day was here at last. She laughed out loud, turning on her stereo to listen to the carols that had been playing all week long. So, this is what it felt like to finally celebrate Christmas. Jane had bought her a small plastic tree so she could decorate it. It stood at three feet and even came with lights.

"It's your tree and you can decorate it with anything. You can get tinsel and crystal balls, shining paper, whatever your heart delights in."

Linda chose to decorate her tree with scripture verses and she had placed it in a corner of the room that she didn't use much, but it was still quite visible from her bed. It would be the last thing she saw before falling asleep and the first when she woke up. Her Christmas tree would never go out all year round. She would replace the verses from time to time, but this season they all spoke about a promise of a Savior, right from Genesis to Revelation. When she had told Allan about how she intended to decorate her tree, he had offered to help her with the Bible verses.

When he brought her about thirty small cards of different colored paper with verses written in beautiful calligraphy, she had nearly wept with gratitude. His kind consideration moved her greatly and she had spent Christmas Eve tying the little notes on her tree. The only ornament she put on the tree was a large gold star that Nancy had found among her own decorations. It was old but still usable, she had said. Linda didn't care, her tree was complete.

She got out of bed and walked to her tree. What she had decided she would be doing every single day for thirty days would be to randomly choose a verse and let it minister to her for the whole day. She closed her eyes, laughing softly and felt around her tree, then touched a card.

"Greater love hath no man than this, that a man should give his life for his friends," she quoted the verse taken from the Gospel of John, the fifteenth chapter and thirteenth verse. Sitting back on her haunches she let the words wash over her and then stood up. She didn't want to be still dressing when Allan came to pick her up.

They were all meeting at the orphanage at nine. Allan would preach a short sermon, then they would hand out their gifts to all the children. Linda had called the warden and obtained the number. There were fifty-five children at the orphanage, so the four of them had pooled their resources together to get them small gifts. They also managed to get something for all the wardens and had spent Christmas Eve at Nancy's house, wrapping them up. Nancy would bring the gifts to the home.

Linda felt so much joy that she was sharing what she had with her little brothers and sisters as she had come to refer to all the children at the orphanage. Given that Terry, the girl she had subleased the bedsitter from had decided to give it up, the rent had decreased. Now she dealt directly with the estate agent in charge of collecting rent. Terry and her boyfriend, Mitch, would be getting married in April and she had even asked Linda to be one of her bridesmaids. It was a great honor for Linda.

With the extra money and whatever she had saved in the months she worked at CCF, Linda had decided to give the little ones a special Christmas. Nancy, Jane and Allan contributed a good amount too and they had enough to buy a nice big Christmas cake. The orphanage would provide a special but simple lunch since they were still in dire financial straits.

When her cellphone rang and she saw a strange number, she almost didn't pick the phone up. "Hello?"

"Linda, I finally got myself a cellphone. Actually, it was a Christmas gift from my mother who's been complaining that I don't communicate enough. The package arrived yesterday. Are you ready?"

"Yes," she said breathlessly. She was going to spend the day with Allan, having fun with the children and away from work. No matter what happened afterwards, she was determined that this was going to be her special day. She would be with the man she loved so deeply.

"We need a special Christmas miracle, like perhaps Allan finally admitting that he's in love with Linda Patterson," Jane said as she maneuvered through the light traffic as they made their way to Precious Gems.

Nancy laughed out loud. "I thought I was growing old and imagining things. So, you noticed it too."

"Yes, actually, almost for four months now. The boy is so protective of Linda that only a blind donkey would fail to see what is going on."

"What about our Linda?"

"The girl is so deeply in love that she glows without knowing it. Love does something to a woman. The other day when I stopped by her office, I found two young men waiting to see her. She was quite puzzled as to why they would seek her out but I understood."

Nancy raised her hands heavenwards. "Dear Lord, today is a day of miracles as started on the first Christmas. Send us a miracle and let these two lovely children finally find their way to each other."

"Amen."

"Does anyone know what is going on?" Peter Banks asked a group of ladies who were standing around the parking lot. Members of the congregation were arriving in droves and nothing seemed to be going on at the church.

In previous years, music would be blaring and caterers would be setting up tents on the front lawn of the church. There would be decorations all over and generally it would be a festive mood all through. Today, however, all was silent. As they were standing around in small groups, five large buses drove into the parking lot, and right behind them came their senior pastor.

Before anyone could ask him anything, he held up his hand. "I know you're all surprised to see that nothing is happening right now, yet it's Christmas Day." There were murmurs of assent. "This year, dear brethren, we're doing things differently. It's not business as usual." Sophia, who was standing beside her husband nodded. "We're taking a trip on this great day and at the end of the day, may the Lord touch our hearts so we really know Who we're celebrating and why we celebrate Him." Surprisingly, there was a loud chorus of 'amen' from the congregation.

"No one is being forced to come with us but I promise that this is going to be a wonderful day. If you're ready for a new adventure, please board the buses. All your cars will be safe as there are people to take care of them." Richard took his wife's hand and led the way, boarding one of the buses. Soon the others joined him, filling four buses. The fifth had a few seats left and they left, singing carols and rejoicing.

Sophia squeezed her husband's hand. "You did the right thing, my darling. I love you so much for who you are."

Richard shook his head, smiling even as he did so. "The Lord led us to do this. And no one will ever get to know what we did. No more showbiz for us, from now on it is the Gospel in all its fullness."

"And I love you even more," she leaned forward and kissed his cheek, unaware that the members of their congregation were watching them. There was loud clapping and Richard grinned at them, pulling his wife close.

10

CELEBRATING A NEW SEASON

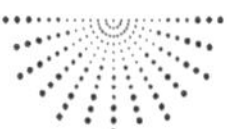

Linda, Allan, Nancy, Jane and the children, as well as the wardens of Precious Gems Children's Home watched with dropping jaws as five large buses drove into the small parking lot, barely fitting in. The doors opened and people poured out, and that's when the group recognized them.

There was a hush as Reverend Clarke and Sophia got off, then walked to where Allan was standing. "We hope it's not too late for us to join in on your Christmas celebrations."

Allan hugged the man who had been like a mentor to him from the moment he arrived in Oklahoma City, even though they'd had their differences. "You're all welcome, though I should be asking Mrs. Winters to do the honors." He introduced Richard and Sophia to the staff of the home and soon everyone was being taken on a tour around the facility.

When they emerged from their brief tour, it was to find two large catering vans with the logo 'Mama's Soul Food' setting up.

"Did you know about this?" Linda whispered to Allan when they got a brief moment together.

He shook his head. "Reverend Clarke is the kind of man who does things that others don't really understand. I can bet you that only Sophia knew about it, given the surprised looks on the faces of people when they got here."

"I can't believe that God has answered my prayer of giving my little brothers and sisters a Christmas they'll never forget. The first Christmas for most of them, like it is for me."

"Our Lord works in mysterious ways. Who knew that something like this could happen?" Before Linda could say anything in response, he was called away by one of the deacons.

Sophia came towards Linda. "Linda, is it?" She nodded. "Could you organize for us to have a place where we can hold a brief service?"

"Of course, Mrs. Clarke. I'll do that right away."

Because they had already been preparing for a service, the hall was ready, though the chairs weren't enough and people had to stand or lean against the walls. Reverend Clarke made all the men stand while ladies and children sat down and after a powerful session of worship, even without instruments, he stood in front of the whole congregation.

"Merry Christmas to you all. It's a wonderful day for us to remember the real reason why we celebrate Christmas. About two thousand years ago, our Savior left His glory and came down to earth. Born in a manger, He lived among the common people, preaching, teaching and healing them. He showed love when people didn't deserve it, much like it is for us today. We don't deserve His love and grace and yet He chooses to extend those gifts to us anyway.

When Sophia and I started out in ministry, we told ourselves that we wouldn't allow power, possessions and pleasure to mar our work for the Lord." He bowed his head and when he raised it again, people were surprised to see tears running down his face. Sophia handed him a handkerchief. "Over the years, we did just that, allowing other things to take the place of our Lord in our lives. We went so far from Him that we soon forgot what celebrations like

Christmas and Easter are. To us, they became days to indulge our carnal desires, show how great we are and we taught others to do the same. It took one strong young man who stood up for the truth and refused to compromise his calling, to make us see our erroneous ways. That's why Sophia and I said that this year it wasn't going to be business as usual. When we read the Gospels about our Lord Jesus, we find out that He came solely to give. He gave of His time, strength and self. He gave His all for us and we ought to learn to do the same. By this shall all men know that ye are my disciples, if you have love one to another. The words of our Lord. Do we love each other? Does the world see us as Christ's disciples because we care for one another?"

By the time Richard concluded his message, everyone was weeping silently. Before he could even make an altar call, people ran to the front, sobbing loudly without a care. There was a time of repentance and finally all was quiet.

"It's been a very emotional time for all of us today but I'm so happy the Lord graciously allowed us to go through this. We are starting over and on behalf of Crossroads Christian Fellowship, we would like to give our love offering of twenty-five thousand dollars to Precious Gems Children's Home." There was stunned surprise before everyone broke out into applause. "Ideally, this money was part of what we received for this year's Christmas celebrations but this is where it should rightly go." More applause. "We also promise that this home is our responsibility now. We'll support you in every way we can, and I'll ask Pastor Allan and Linda to organize so that every two months, at least one group from church will come for a visit. You belong to us and we belong to you."

"Amen!" Everyone including the children who could, chorused.

"I've never seen such joy on the faces of our congregation," Allan told Linda as he drove her home later that day after the festivities. "I've been so wrong about everyone and it makes me feel deeply ashamed. God can touch hearts and people change."

"My first Christmas; this has been even beyond what I prayed for. My family at Precious Gems can now sleep better because that donation will go a long way in solving a number of the problems they have."

"You and I are charged with the task of the bi-monthly visits. I know that we'll be taking more donations to them, and, God willing, when we celebrate the next Christmas, there'll be testimonies from the children, wardens and also members of our congregation."

Linda was surprised when Allan got to her apartment and instead of opening the door for her, he restrained her. "Linda, there's something I've been meaning to tell you. I thought we would spend the day with the little ones, then leave early so I could take you out to dinner."

"Dinner, why?"

"Because, dear girl, I needed private time with you. Ever since you came to CCF, we've been together in missions, intercession and even work. I found out that you're the woman I've been praying for."

"What do you mean?" She put a hand to her heart. It was racing as though she'd just run a marathon.

"Linda," he took her hands. "What I mean is that I love you, have loved you for a while and I was wondering how to bring this up without sounding like I'm taking advantage of our meetings." She didn't know what to say. "We have the same calling in ministry and two can only walk together when they be agreed."

"Allan …" Linda couldn't believe that he was declaring his love for her. "I don't know what to say."

"Say you love me, those are the only words that I really long to hear from you. My darling, am I chasing a dream or should I have hope?"

"Allan, are you sure about what you're saying?"

His answer was to extract a small box from his jacket pocket. "I've been walking around with this ring for days, trying to gather the courage to ask you to marry me. Open it."

Linda did. It was a small gold ring with a diamond. "Oh! It's beautiful."

"Here, let me," he slipped it onto her finger. It was a perfect fit. "I guessed your size and got it right," he touched her cheek. "See how good we are for each other?"

"It's really beautiful," Linda had never received such an expensive gift before.

"But not as beautiful as the woman I love. If only she would tell me that she loves me too."

Linda giggled, "What if she doesn't?"

"Then I'll be forced to kiss her into submission." He lowered his head and she moved back.

"My neighbors are watching," she pushed him away. "Okay, I concede. I do love you, Allan. So much that it's terrifying."

"That's my girl. Now, go into your apartment before I change my mind about kissing you. I'll come and take you for a picnic tomorrow so we can talk about how we're going to break the news of our engagement to Jane and Nancy, and the rest of the congregation."

"I'm sure they already know or suspect something, because today Jane was making some subtle comments to me which I chose to ignore because I thought she was wrong or imagining things."

"She'll be glad to know that she wasn't. Now, my darling, get out of my car and remember that I really do love you."

"And I love you too," she leaned towards him and gave him a gentle kiss on his lips then opened the car door and got out.

Allan watched her walking away, a gentle smile on his face. She turned around and waved, the joy on her face quite evident. Allan waved back before starting his car and driving off. This had been a wonderful day indeed. He was loved and he loved. That was a beautiful feeling.

Thank you so much for reading. We hope you really enjoyed the story. Please consider leaving a positive review on Amazon if you did.